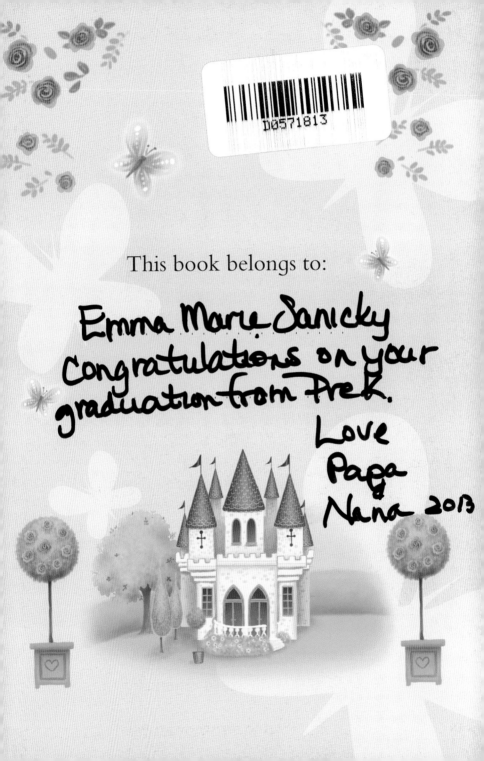

This book belongs to:

Emma Marie Janicky
Congratulations on your
graduation from PreK.
Love
Papa
Nana 2013

Reading Together

This story is written in a special way so that a child and an adult can 'take turns' in reading the text.

The left hand side is for the adult to read.

Once upon a time there was a merchant who had three daughters.
The youngest daughter was called Beauty. They all lived in the country.
One day the merchant had to go into the town.
Beauty asked her father to bring her a pink rose.

Beauty asked her father to bring her a pink rose

The right hand side has a simple sentence (taken from the story) which the child reads.

Firstly, it is always helpful to read the whole book to your child, stopping to talk about the pictures. Explain that you are going to read it again but this time the child can join in.

Read the left hand page and when you come to the sentence which is repeated on the other page run your finger under this. Your child then tries to read the same sentence opposite.

Searching for the child's sentence in the adult version is a useful activity. Your child will have a real sense of achievement when all the sentences on the right hand page can be read. Giving lots of praise is very important.

Enjoy the story together.

I Can Read...

Beauty and the Beast

Once upon a time there was a merchant
who had three daughters.
The youngest daughter was called
Beauty. They all lived in the country.
One day the merchant had to go into
the town.
Beauty asked her father to bring her
a pink rose.

Beauty asked her father to bring
her a pink rose.

The merchant went to town.
On the way back it started to rain.
The merchant got lost in the woods.
The merchant found a huge old castle.
He went inside.

The merchant got lost in the woods.

There was no one in the castle. But there was dinner on the table and a warm fire. The merchant ate the food and went to sleep.

When he woke up he remembered that he had promised to take Beauty a rose.

There was no one in the castle.

The merchant went into the garden
of the castle. He picked a pink rose.
The merchant heard a loud roar.
He saw a huge, ugly beast.
"That is my rose!" said the Beast.

The merchant heard a loud roar.

The merchant said he was sorry.
He explained that the rose was a present
for Beauty.
"I will spare your life if Beauty will
come and live with me," said the Beast.

The merchant said he was sorry.

When the merchant got home he told
Beauty what had happened.
Beauty said she would go and live
in the castle.
When Beauty met the Beast she
was surprised.
He was kind to her. Beauty and the
Beast soon became friends.

Beauty and the Beast soon
became friends.

Beauty missed her father and sisters.
The Beast said she could go home.
Beauty promised she would only stay at
home for a week.
But Beauty liked being at home so
much she forgot her promise.
Beauty did not go back to the castle.

Beauty did not go back to the castle.

One night Beauty had a dream.
Beauty dreamed that the Beast was
very ill.
She hurried back to the castle.
The Beast was dying of a broken heart
because he missed Beauty so much.

Beauty dreamed that the Beast
was very ill.

Beauty realised she loved the Beast. She started to cry. Her tears fell on the Beast's face. WHOOSH!
The Beast was changed into a handsome Prince.

The Beast was changed into
a handsome Prince.

The prince explained that a wicked fairy
had put a spell on him. The spell turned the
prince into the Beast.
Beauty's tears had broken the spell.
Beauty and the Prince fell in love.
They lived happily ever after in the castle.

Beauty and the Prince fell in love.

Key Words

Can you read these words and find them in the book?

merchant

rose

Beauty

Beast

castle

Questions and Answers

Now that you've read the story can you answer these questions?

a. Who asked her father to bring her a pink rose?

b. Whose meal did the merchant eat in the castle?

c. Where did Beauty go to live with the Beast?

a. Beauty   b. The Beast's meal   c. The castle

Tell your own Story

Can you make up a different story
with the pictures and words below?

house

merchant

woods

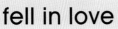

sisters

Beast

horse

fell in love

castle

Mix and Match

Draw a line from the pictures to the
correct word to match them up.

rose

Beast

castle

Beauty

merchant

horse